DOG DIARIES

SUSAN

DOG DIARIES

#1: Ginger
A puppy-mill survivor in search of a *furever* family

#2: Buddy
The first Seeing Eye guide dog

#3: Barry
Legendary rescue dog of the Great Saint Bernard Hospice

#4: Togo
Unsung hero of the 1925 Nome Serum Run

#5: Dash
One of two dogs to travel to the New World aboard the *Mayflower*

#6: Sweetie
George Washington's "perfect" foxhound

#7: Stubby
One of the greatest dogs in military history

#8: Fala
"Assistant" to President Franklin Delano Roosevelt

#9: Sparky
Fire dog veteran of the Great Chicago Fire

#10: Rolf
A tripod therapy dog

#11: Tiny Tim
Canine companion to Charles Dickens, author of *A Christmas Carol*

#12: Susan
Matriarch of Queen Elizabeth II's corgi dynasty

DOG DIARIES

SUSAN

BY KATE KLIMO • ILLUSTRATED BY TIM JESSELL

RANDOM HOUSE 🏠 NEW YORK

Text copyright © 2018 by Kate Klimo
Cover art and interior illustrations copyright © 2018 by Tim Jessell
Photographs courtesy of Lisa Sheridan/Hulton Royals Collection/Getty Images, p. ix;
Everett Collection Inc./Alamy Stock Photo, p. 146; PA Images/Alamy Stock Photo,
pp. 147, 148, 149; © Jessica Klein, courtesy of Roberta Ludlow, p. 150

Visit us on the Web! rhcbooks.com

Educators and librarians, for a variety of teaching tools, visit us at
RHTeachersLibrarians.com

Library of Congress Cataloging-in-Publication Data
Names: Klimo, Kate, author. | Jessell, Tim, illustrator.
Title: Susan / by Kate Klimo ; illustrated by Tim Jessell.
Description: First edition. | New York : Random House, [2018] | Series: Dog diaries ; 12 |
Summary: "Susan—the corgi presented to Princess Elizabeth on her eighteenth birthday—
reveals secrets of life in Buckingham Palace"—Provided by publisher. Includes historical notes
and information about the breed.
Identifiers: LCCN 2016057333 (print) | LCCN 2017028192 (ebook) |
ISBN 978-1-5247-1964-7 (trade pbk.) | ISBN 978-1-5247-1965-4 (lib. bdg.) |
ISBN 978-1-5247-1966-1 (ebook)
Subjects: LCSH: Pembroke Welsh corgi—Juvenile fiction. | CYAC: Pembroke Welsh corgi—
Fiction. | Dogs—Fiction. | Elizabeth II, Queen of Great Britain, 1926– —Fiction. |
Kings, queens, rulers, etc.—Fiction. | England—Fiction.
Classification: LCC PZ10.3.K686 (ebook) | LCC PZ10.3.K686 Sus 2018 (print) |
DDC [Fic]—dc23

Printed in the United States of America

10 9 8 7 6 5 4 3 2 1

First Edition

For Roberta and her boys
— K.K.

For Dad, who loves his corgi . . .
except for the shedding
—T.J.

CONTENTS

Ten-year-old Princess Elizabeth and Dookie ("a born sentimentalist"), from the 1936 book *Our Princesses and Their Dogs* by Michael Chance

Before My Time

In the kennel where I was born, the story has been passed down from mum to pup for generations. And even though it took place before I was born, I have heard it told so many times that it is written upon my heart.

Once upon a time, there was a little girl named Thelma. She was nine years old when her dog was accidentally run over by a motorcar. Mind you, this was no ordinary accident. The motorcar happened to be driven by the Duke of York, the man who would one day be king of England. But our Thelma didn't care a fig about that. All she knew was that she had lost her beloved friend, the light of her life. And her heart was broken.

The duke, as you can imagine, felt terrible. With deepest sympathies, he wrote to Thelma's parents and offered to purchase a new dog for the family. Her parents felt Thelma was too grief-stricken to accept another dog. Ever so politely, they turned down the duke's generous offer and let Thelma know that they had done so. After a few months, when Thelma's heart had mended, she wrote the duke a letter. She'd take that new dog now, thank you very much, she told him. But the duke, not wanting to go against the parents' original wishes, declined to make good on his offer.

There would be no new dog for Thelma at this time. But she soldiered on and eventually grew up to be one of the most famous dog breeders in all of England. At the kennel she founded—known as Rozavel—she raised many a prizewinner. Among them were Alsatians, Scotties, Airedales, chow chows, and Chihuahuas. But her very favorite breed was the corgi. And while she didn't, strictly speaking, *discover* corgis, her work did go a long way toward making us famous and getting us officially recognized by the Kennel Club.

Thelma encountered her first corgi as a young gal on holiday in Wales. From the window of her roadster, she saw one dashing across a field on his short but sturdy legs, expertly herding cattle by nipping at their heels. Welsh farmers had been breeding corgis to herd for hundreds of years.

What did we herd? Anything that needed herding: sheep, geese, ducks, horses, cattle, sometimes even the farmers' wayward children. It was from these same farmers that Thelma purchased the very finest specimens of our kind, with an eye to starting her own line. At Rozavel, she set about breeding two types of corgis: the Pembroke Welsh corgi (smaller and with a naturally bobbed tail) and the Cardigan Welsh corgi (bigger than the Pembroke and with a long tail).

So successful was she in her efforts in the 1930s that her Pem stud, Red Dragon, became quite the dog-about-town. Thelma sold one of his excellent pups to a member of the royal family, Viscount Weymouth. Now, the viscount's children happened to be playmates with the young princesses Elizabeth and Margaret Rose—the daughters of the very same Duke of York who had crossed paths with Thelma as a child! The young princesses were so smitten with the viscount's corgi that they begged their father for one of their own. In short order, the duke summoned Thelma to his residence. She came bearing three charming Pembroke Welsh corgi pups, from which the children were to pick one.

Did Thelma let on to the duke that she was the same little girl whose dog he had run over all those years ago? Like a mysterious stranger in a fairy tale, she chose to keep her identity a secret. After all, that had been a lifetime ago. In *this* lifetime, breeding superb dogs and finding outstanding homes for them were what interested her.

Naturally, the princesses wanted to keep all three of the pups. But that was not going to happen. Not even princesses get to have *everything* they wish for. So after much snuggling and soul-searching and royal dithering, they chose Rozavel Golden Eagle. The way I heard it, Golden Eagle became so stuck-up and full of himself from being the pet of princesses that the staff took to calling him "the Duke." The girls, delighted with the nickname, dubbed him Dookie. Three years later, Dookie was joined by a second corgi from Thelma's kennel, Lady Jane. Lady Jane and Elizabeth—known as Lilibet to those nearest and dearest—soon became inseparable. The most adorable little book titled *Our Princesses and Their Dogs* came out just in time for Christmas 1936. It was a picture book full of photographs of Elizabeth and Margaret Rose frolicking with their beloved corgis and other royal dogs.

The same month of the book's publication, the Duke of York ascended to the throne of England. When the people of England looked upon the pictures in this book, they saw a family with a keen attachment to and understanding of dogs. They knew that their king was a fine master, a good father, and a gentle man. Thanks in part to dogs, the people of England welcomed with open arms their new king, George VI.

Three years later, in 1939, a terrible war broke out between England and Germany. Enemy bombs fell throughout the land, destroying property and taking lives. As an example to their subjects, the king and queen chose to remain in London in the royal residence, Buckingham Palace. The princesses were sent off to the country, to Windsor Castle, behind whose stout stone walls they were kept safe. Watching over them were the officers of the Grenadier Guards, whose job it is to protect the royal family—and the royal corgis as well, although by now there was just one. Dookie had died of old age at the start of the war. Fortunately, Thelma found a mate for Lady Jane, and she soon gave birth to Crackers.

These were trying times for the nation. One bomb fell on Buckingham Palace, destroying the chapel and, very nearly, the royal couple themselves. When the king and queen were not in London, they were traveling by train throughout their battle-torn country. They greeted troops and called upon injured soldiers in hospitals in an effort to buck up morale.

Meanwhile, back at Windsor Castle, the princesses were snug as two dear little bugs in a rug, for the castle was frightfully well fortified. In addition to being patrolled by the Grenadier Guards and soldiers armed with antiaircraft guns, it was surrounded by barbed wire. The windows were blacked out so that lights in the castle were not

visible to enemy aircraft at night. Food and even bathwater were in short supply. The princesses didn't sleep upstairs in their bedrooms but, instead, deep underground in a bombproof bunker beneath the castle tower. *Imagine!*

Did the princesses utter a word of complaint over their plight? Not a bit! There was work to be done. Bandages to roll for the wounded. Teas and luncheons to prepare for the soldiers. That Stiff Upper Lip, for which the British are known the world over, had to be maintained even in, and perhaps *especially* in, trying times.

Lady Jane and Crackers did their parts, too. I daresay no more stalwart corgis ever drew breath. When the princesses missed their parents or flinched at the whistle and scream of an exploding bomb, the corgis were there to offer a warm lick and a furry hug.

Which makes this next part of the story all the more painful to tell. But tell it I must.

One day, Lilibet was out walking on the grounds with Jane. Windsor Castle is surrounded by a vast tract of fields and woodlands known as Windsor Great Park. And it was not uncommon for the corgis to run loose without a leash within the safety of the park. But on that unhappy day, from out of nowhere, a park ranger came along in his vehicle. He failed to see the small red dog standing in his path. Jane was killed instantly.

It is bad enough to run over someone's pet. But when that pet happens to be the beloved companion of a member of the royal family? Just imagine how the poor lad felt! Mumbling his deepest apologies, he took Jane's broken body away to prepare it for burial. Meanwhile, Lilibet marched off to the castle and up to her room. You might think that she threw herself down on her bed and wept and wailed for her lost dog. But you would be mistaken.

Missing not a beat, the princess sat down at her desk and wrote a letter to the young ranger. She urged him not to feel badly for what had happened. She was sure it was not his fault. These things happen, and one must pull up one's socks and get on with one's life as best one can. Righty-ho!

Do you see what was happening here? She, the one who had suffered the loss, was reaching out to comfort the one who had inflicted it.

Had I been out in the park that day with Lilibet and Lady Jane, would I have been so kind and forgiving? I rather think not. Instead of receiving a letter of forgiveness from me, that ranger would have gotten a sharp nip on the heel! In my experience, most humans need to be kept in line, like so many naughty sheep or cattle.

But that, as they say, is neither here nor there. What is important about this event, tragic though it may have been, was that it gave rise to Lilibet's receiving, on the occasion of her eighteenth birthday, a new corgi to replace the one she had lost.

And that corgi, dear girls and boys, was I.

MY LITTLE LADY

I was born during the war, in the year 1944, registered under the name Hickathrift Pippa. A long name for a short dog, you're thinking. Perhaps that's why Thelma decided to call me Sue—for short, so to speak. She suggested to Princess Elizabeth, the day she introduced us, that she do the same. But the princess had ideas of her own.

"We'll call you Susan," she whispered in my

ear. "You and I are going to get along famously."

At only two months of age, I was barely enough to fill her hands. But what hands they were, gentle and sure, like her voice. And in her lovely eyes, sparks danced like fairy lights. She knew me for what I was, which is to say, a little bit enchanted and a little bit wild.

There is a story told in Wales, and it goes like this: Two little girls were playing in a meadow when they came upon a nest of corgi pups. With their deep red coats and their sharp muzzles and pointed ears, the girls mistook them for abandoned fox kits. They brought the orphaned kits home to show their parents. But the parents said, "Daughters, those aren't foxes. Those are enchanted dogs visiting from the fairy kingdom. Fairy warriors ride on their backs. They pull the coaches of the fairy

princesses. If you look very closely, you will see
on their fur the pale imprint of fairy saddles and
harnesses."

I believe that Lilibet saw in me the faint ev-
idence of the fairy world. And as for me, I had

found my own life-size fairy princess in Lilibet. Although I would never grow big enough to pull her royal carriage, I could serve as her loyal companion, her comfort in times of strife, her guardian against all enemies, and her furry champion. She was my little lady. And I, for that matter, was hers.

In those days, Lilibet and Margaret Rose and their girlfriends belonged to a Girl Guide troop. (The American scouting group was called Girl Scouts.) The war kept the princesses and their troop on their toes. I'd follow Lilibet as she bustled about the enormous castle kitchen. Some days, she baked cookies and scones. Other days, she brewed hearty soups and stews. When the bombs fell on London, refugees swarmed into the countryside, hungry and homeless. Food, as I have already said, was in short supply and what little there was, people obtained with slips of paper called ration coupons. Lilibet and her troop greeted the refugees with food and blankets and kind words. And after she had seen to the needs of her grateful countrymen, she stood at the sink—up to her elbows in suds—and washed the dishes. Surely, no princess of any kingdom had ever worked so hard for her people.

After chores were done, Lilibet liked to take a turn about the grounds. The castle property was dotted with the loveliest ponds. How I adored to wade and splash about in them. I was a bit of a wild girl in those moments, paddling among the froggies and turtles and funny little ducks that sprinted away from my snapping jaws. I'd drive those ducks out of the pond and herd them back and forth along the bank. This was my idea of utter blissikins!

Far less blissful were our visits to the stables. It

was there that I learned a bitter truth: I was not, after all, Lilibet's one and only furry friend. There were others. And these others were horses. Her love of horses was very *nearly* as great as her love for me. Her jacket pockets stuffed with horse biscuits, she would walk up and down the aisle of the stable and give each beast a treat. Stroking their long silky noses, she called each one by name. Even the mightiest of them bowed low and nickered as they laid their huge noses in her tiny hand and sucked up the biscuits.

Watch yourself! I warned them.

What are you on about, you runty little rascal? one of them said, flushing biscuit crumbs from his nostrils.

Watch you don't nip her fingertips with those great clunking gnashers of yours.

You think we can't tell a finger from a biscuit, do

you? If you had eyes in your silly little head, you'd see that our gnashers never touch her fingers. It's all done with the lips. We horses have very talented lips.

Is that so? Well, watch this! I turned to Lilibet and let out a sharp little bark.

"Here you go, Susan!" Lilibet said, breaking off half a biscuit and tossing it to me. I leapt in the air and caught it in my teeth. *How do you like that for lightning reflexes?* I said to the horse as I crunched up my own treat.

But, oh, how I dreaded the inevitable moment when she would remove one of these brutes from its stall and lead it out into the stable yard. These horses had absurdly long legs. They were legs that just did not know when to quit. In those days, she favored a particularly long-legged steed named Sir Kay. I paced back and forth as she brushed him and crooned to him and polished him like some great bronze statue. Why couldn't she ask a groom to handle this chore? She was, after all, a princess. But alas, she actually enjoyed grooming her own mounts. Tacking them up as well. After a great deal of brushing and fussing, she tossed a saddle on his back, buckled a bit and bridle on, and climbed on top of the beast.

Sir Kay looked down upon me and snorted.

Am I not a splendid specimen of horseflesh? In some other age, I would have ridden into battle with a knight in armor on my back. Now I carry a princess no heavier than a feather.

I growled. *See that you trod carefully and give her a smooth and safe ride.*

He pawed at the cobbles. *Pishposh. She and her sister have been riding us since they were old enough to walk.*

I knew that. But I also knew that, as Lilibet's

guardian and champion, it was my job to assure her safety and well-being. Riding horses was dangerous. Unfortunately, my little lady was never happier than when she was in the saddle. Chin lifted, back straight, Lilibet took up the reins and urged Sir Kay forward.

Wait for me! I called out as I ran to catch up.

"Step lively, Susan. And watch the hooves!" Lilibet warned.

Righty-ho! A more fearful mistress might have

left me back at the castle. But Lilibet was tough and smart and quick, and she expected the same from me. Who was I to let her down?

As the horse strode out of the stable and onto the bridle path, I dashed at his heels to herd him. But unlike a cow or a sheep, this animal defied herding. In fact, he had rather a mind of his own! He reared up and galloped off into the woods with Lilibet clinging to his neck like a limpet. By the time I caught up, Lilibet had hauled on the reins

and gotten the wicked beast in hand.

"He has spirit, this one," she said breathlessly, her eyes bright and her cheeks rosy.

The spirit of the devil, said I, snarling at the horse.

Don't look at me. She likes a bit of a challenge, said the arrogant steed. *And unlike the other humans, she refuses to wear a helmet. She's fearless, this one. Thinks she's indestructible, she does.*

She might be fearless, but riding without a helmet was most ill advised. I had seen other humans riding horses. They all wore hard hats. But Lilibet wore nothing but a flimsy head scarf tied beneath her chin.

Watch yourself, I warned the horse. *Or else.*

Or else what? Bite me with your tiny teeth? HA! Try it, and I'll kick you into the next county. I am no docile cow. I'm a sleek and noble Thoroughbred. My ancestors carried kings and warriors. Respect must be paid.

It took me some doing, but in time, I and Sir Kay—and his stablemates—arrived at an understanding. I wouldn't nip at them. And they wouldn't hurt Lilibet. I learned to weave in and out between their hooves. They learned to watch where they were setting them down. But here's a fact about horses. They are not to be trusted. For all their size, they can be the most shameless cowards. Sometimes all it took was a grouse darting across their path to frighten them senseless.

Once, when her horse spooked, he flung Lilibet clear off his back. Flying high into the air, she came back to earth with a dull thud. There she lay on her back, as still as a doll. I ran over, barking frantically, and licked her face. Her eyes opened. She blinked. Then she sat up and dusted herself off. "No harm done," said she as she stood and climbed back onto the treacherous beast.

Sir Kay was right. She was fearless.

Perhaps it was this very fearlessness that led her to want to do something more for the war effort than baking cakes and making soup. She started traveling, every day, to the Mechanical Transport Training Center in the nearby town of Camberley. There, she got lessons on how to drive big lorries. (Americans call them trucks.) First big horses. Then big lorries. My Lilibet did things on a grand scale!

In this new life, she was known as Second Subaltern Elizabeth Alexandra Mary Windsor, reporting daily for duty in her crisp uniform. Not only did she drive lorries through the crowded and twisty streets of Surrey, but she learned to change flat tires and spark plugs, and take an engine apart and put it back together again. Many was the night when my little lady came home to me with her face smudged with grease. Lilibet was a great deal like me: happiest when she was running around and doing things.

While she was off tinkering with trucks, it was just me and Margaret Rose and the staff banging about the castle. Most of the staff were very kind. But there was this one footman. He was sweetness and light to me whenever Lilibet was about. But the moment she was gone, he kicked me whenever he found me underfoot.

"Out of my way, you spoiled little lapdog!" he muttered.

The nerve! If there's anything that drives me round the twist, it's people who take pleasure in pushing defenseless dogs around. As it happened, I was not without defenses. I left more than my share of tooth marks in the ankle of that villain. Still, you'll be happy to know that he did not serve the household for very long before he was given the sack. I often thought there should have been a sign posted at the servants' entrance: DOG LOVERS ONLY NEED APPLY.

On May 8, 1945, when I was one year old, Victory in Europe Day was declared. It marked the official surrender of the Germans and the end of the war in Europe following nearly six grueling years.

We left Windsor Castle and returned to London. I had been born into wartime, and war was all I knew. But now I sensed something new in the air. It was called peace! The city streets teemed with joyful people celebrating the end of the war. At Buckingham Palace, Lilibet and I joined her sister and parents on the balcony. With us was the funniest little man, who called himself Churchill. He was frightfully important, the prime minister and leader of the English government. He seemed fond of my little lady, so I tolerated him even though he reeked of Cat. People! They can't all be dog lovers, can they? Although they should be. How much finer a place would the world be then? Rather!

That night, Lilibet donned her crisp uniform and left the palace along with her sister. Outside the gates, the streets echoed with music and voices raised in song. Inside the palace, the servants were having their own celebration, raising glasses and passing around trays of food.

Wherever there are trays of food, I may be found. You'd be surprised how much food drops off trays onto the floor. Eventually, the servants all drifted to bed and left me to clean up the last of the crumbs. Near dawn, while the crowds outside still milled about and celebrated and cheered, Lilibet came back to me.

I have a tail. It is quite short. So short, some say, as to be invisible. But they would be wrong. It may not be much, but it's enough for me to wag. And wag it I did every time my little lady came through the door.

"I danced all night, Susan!" she said as she held me in her arms and we watched the sun rise outside the window. "Imagine! I was out there, among all those people, and not a one of them recognized me. I was just another face in the crowd!"

Even then I knew that she was not Just Another Face. She was *the* Face. The Face of England. And one day she would also be the trusty Shepherd of Its People. Do you see now why she and I were so very well suited to one another?

Born herders, the both of us. Quite!

Prince Charming

My little lady met her prince more than four years before I was born. So while I was tempted to resent him as an upstart and an intruder, His Royal Highness Prince Philip of Greece and Denmark was here first. The Greeks had booted Philip's family out of Greece. Unlike the English, the Greeks didn't care to have a monarchy. So he was a prince without a throne, a man without a country and all but penniless. He was not the prince Lilibet's parents would have chosen for her. He was tall and handsome and strong and proud. He was rather like a Thoroughbred: long-legged and ever so full of himself. No surprise, Lilibet fell madly in love. I will say this about him: he had the good sense to love her back.

As the story goes, Lilibet was just a girl when she first set eyes on Philip at a family wedding in 1934. In 1939, she saw him again when she and her parents visited the naval college where he was studying to be an officer. They became pen pals and kept in touch. Later, during the war, when he wasn't on duty, he was a regular visitor at Windsor Castle. Lilibet was always over the moon to see him, and he, her. As for me, I could hear him coming from clear across the city, zooming toward the palace in his sporty roadster.

Was he as pleased to see me? One might say

that corgis were not as precious to Philip as they were to my princess. Philip was a big man who liked big dogs: Labrador retrievers and other great slobbering hounds. The prince and I circled each other warily. He didn't want me to bite him. I didn't want him to break my little lady's heart.

While Philip finished his tour of duty in some far-off land, Lilibet and I spent the summer in Scotland at Balmoral, yet another of the royal residences. It was there that I made myself a couple of new friends. You'll be surprised to learn that they were horses.

They certainly didn't look like any horses *I* had ever seen. They were ponies, actually. Fell ponies, to be exact. Their legs were quite short. Not as short as mine, mind you, but much shorter than the Thoroughbreds' at Windsor. They didn't act like horses, either, all hoity-toity and above it all.

They were regular blokes, descended from the pack animals that once hauled loads from the lead mines to the seaports.

The first time Lilibet swung a saddle onto one of them, he said to me, *Let's have a race, shall we, wee doggie?* His name was Jock. As fast as my little legs could carry me, this wee doggie dashed after Jock as Lilibet galloped him over the moors. He won the first race. I won the second.

You're a fleet-footed little thing, Jock said to me when we were back at the stables and Lilibet was giving him a brisk brushing.

Righty-ho, said I. *I was bred to chase down and herd cattle.*

Done much of that herding lately, my darling? the cheeky pony asked.

I dipped my head. *No. Not really,* I said. *Mostly I herd the princess.*

A princess herder, is it now? He tossed back his head and snorted. *That's a new one on me. Did you hear that, Hans?* he said to the pony in the nearest stall. *This one says she herds princesses.*

Saucy Hans joined in the merriment. *It's a devilish tough job, I hear,* he said. *But* somebody *has to do it. Wouldn't want them wild princesses stampeding all over the countryside, would we now? There'd be mass hysteria, I wager.*

I couldn't help but laugh along with them. That Jock and Hans: what a couple of wags.

The war ending had lifted a great weight off England and the royal family. With her mum and dad, my lady picnicked on the moors. Still, I could tell, Lilibet missed her prince.

That autumn, we returned to London. The streets rang with the sounds of hammers and saws as the city built itself up from the rubble of wartime. In Buckingham Palace, Lilibet and I had our own posh suite of rooms. She now had her own staff: two ladies-in-waiting, a page, and a maid, in addition to Margaret MacDonald, also known as Bobo. Bobo was her lady's maid, taking care of all her personal needs, such as her hair, her clothing, and her bath.

And who took care of me and *my* personal needs? Lilibet—that's who! It was she who fed me and groomed me daily with a special brush she

kept in her desk drawer. She checked me for fleas.
(Yes, those of us who dwell in palaces are not above
getting fleas.) She made sure that my teeth were
healthy and sparkling. She protected my tender
paw pads from injury. She had the most cunning
little magnet, which she used to pick up any loose
pins Bobo might have accidentally left behind after
a dress fitting.

One blustery spring day, she happened to be grooming me when my ears pricked up at the familiar sound of the sporty black roadster roaring up the drive. It was the prince himself, returning from the war. Lilibet dropped my brush and bounded off to meet him. So much for my grooming.

Later that evening, they had dinner together up in our rooms with Crawfie, her Scottish nanny, and myself as chaperones. It would be the first of many such cozy get-togethers. He looked frightfully large and masculine wedged into our fuzzy pink drawing room. But here they had something they would rarely find outside the palace walls: peace and quiet and privacy.

Philip wasn't the only man who claimed Lilibet's attentions in those days. Her dear papa, the king, was ever so eager to spend time with her. He would invite her on long walks with him to discuss the business of government and politics and the crown, which he called the Royal Firm. If you have not already guessed, let me make this clear: Lilibet was a serious young woman, educated by some of the finest minds in the realm. And she adored the company of the king, very nearly as much as she enjoyed mine. Fortunately, the king was as big a dog lover as his daughter, so I never felt less than welcome in his presence.

At night, when we were alone together, Lilibet fretted. Working for the Royal Firm required long hours, much travel, and a world of worry. It was taking a toll on her father's health. He looked gray and thin and smelled of the cigarettes his physicians urged him to quit smoking. He asked Elizabeth to go with him on a tour of South Africa and Rhodesia. "We're traveling by royal yacht," she explained to me as she prepared to depart. "I'm afraid you'd get awfully seasick if you came along."

Did I ask to tag along? I was a bit of a homebody, and I never doubted for a moment that my little lady would eventually return to me. In the meantime, I was busy with the business of the Corgi Firm. There were maids and footmen needing constant herding, up and down the halls and the great staircases. There were gardens to patrol for birds and vermin. There were roaring vacuum cleaning machines to supervise. And legions of mice to be flushed from their cover behind costly tapestries and drapes.

After three months, my little lady returned home. My tail practically wagged *me*, I was so chuffed to see her. And she arrived bursting with the good news.

A royal wedding was in the offing!

A Fairy-Tale Wedding

A ball was held at Buckingham Palace to celebrate the royal engagement of Princess Elizabeth and Prince Philip. People from all over the world attended. I would have loved to take a spin or two across the dance floor, but I, alas, was not on the guest list. From up in our suite, I could hear people laughing and singing and chattering. I heard the rhythmic thumping and laughter that told me the king himself was leading a long conga line through the staterooms down below. How I longed to be at the head of that line! Can corgies conga, you ask? One, two, three, kick! You can bet your dance shoes on that, boys and girls.

On the morning of the wedding, in November of 1947, Bobo and the other ladies assisted the princess in donning her wedding gown. Cloth and thread, like food and drink, were still in short supply. Elizabeth had to use ration coupons to obtain some of the fabric she needed to make her dress and train. I like to think, as the companion of a princess, that I had a feel for such things as gowns and balls and precious gems. The garment itself was the creation of the Court Designer. Made of soft white satin decorated with crystals and seed pearls, it had a thirteen-foot-long train of ivory silk and a veil of tulle that was to be attached to her head by a jeweled tiara belonging to her grandmum, Queen Mary. But just as they were attaching the veil to her head, the tiara broke!

Horrors! A royal bride without a tiara. Rarely had I seen my little lady so put out. Fortunately, the Court Jeweler was standing by. Police officers escorted him to his shop. He repaired the tiara and returned it to the palace in short order. Crisis averted! The wedding proceeded.

Before she left the palace, Lilibet knelt down

and held my face in her hands. "Soon, Susan, I'll be a married woman. But you're not to worry. I'll always have time for you."

I should jolly well hope so. I knew this much: I would always have time for her.

Off she swept, in her dazzling gown. After she left, the palace fell into a dull silence, as if Lilibet had taken all the life and sparkle with her. I confess I would have known very little of the wedding itself were it not for a chance meeting with a certain feathered creature.

The footman had taken me out to the garden for my afternoon walk. The poor lad shifted from foot to foot, his breath streamy in the damp and freezing air. I was poking my nose into a bed of thyme when the creature in question alighted nearby on the branch of an ancient mulberry. She fluffed her wings.

I'd seen this one before. She was one of those Trafalgar Square pigeons. Some humans adored and fed them. Others found them dirty and irritating. I belonged to the latter camp. Normally, I would have given chase. But today I had other uses for her. You see, unlike we four-legged earthbound types, birds fly everywhere and see everything.

I say, there, Madam Pigeon! I called to her. *Might I have a word with you? The name's Susan.*

My mates call me Windy, she said.

Lovely to meet you, Windy. I don't suppose you happened to catch sight of the royal wedding happening across town?

She crooked her neck and fixed me with a beady eye. *A bit hard to miss, wasn't it, luv? Why, I see you've even got crowds here outside the palace.*

It was true. On the other side of the palace gates, people had been gathering since the night before. *They certainly are a noisy enough lot,* I said.

Windy said, *This ain't nothin'. You should see the crowds over at Westminster Abbey. Thousands of folks, I tell you, lining the streets and milling about outside the doors. All of them, just standing there in the bitter cold, waiting to catch a glimpse of the bride and groom. Being in a festive mood, people brought all sorts of tasty tea and cakes. Me and my mates were treated to a regular wedding feast of crumbs.*

Jolly good for you, I said. *But what of the bride and groom? Did you see them?*

First I saw the princess and her father, His Majesty, the king. They arrived in a fancy coach. When them great doors swung open, dashed if there weren't even more people waiting inside. Very important people, too, from the looks of their fancy plumage. Anyway, the crowd outside continued to wait whilst inside, the ceremony went on and on. You know these royals. Love their traditions, they do. The folks wait-ing seemed happy enough, in spite of the weather. Af-ter the ceremony, bride and groom, hand in hand, led the guests down the aisle and out onto the street. The roar from that crowd! I've never heard the like. Re-member, these are the people who have gone without the bare necessities. For six whole years, no good food, no new clothes, and no jobs. This wedding turned out to be just the ticket. The pick-me-up they needed to put them back on their feet.

And the princess? How did she look? I asked Windy.

Downright radiant, in my humble opinion, said Windy. *Then the happy couple stepped into one of them glass coaches. Right out of a fairy tale, it was. They're on their way back here as I speak, escorted by a full military parade in full uniform and spit-polished. I never did see the like, I tell you.*

At that moment, the crowds outside Buckingham Palace's gates exploded in a chorus of loud huzzahs.

That must be them now, I said, my tail wagging.

The footman tugged on my leash. He was shivering like a Chihuahua, poor lad. It must be difficult weathering the winter without benefit of fur. "Come along, Sue," he urged me. "Her ladyship's arrived. Let's get you back indoors."

Windy lifted her wings. *Nice chatting with you, luv. It's back to Trafalgar Square for me.* And off she flew, my fine feathered friend.

Now I am, by nature, an excited sort. But this night, there was extra excitement in the air. And I fed upon it like braised calves' liver. Maybe it was the crowds outside chanting, "We want Elizabeth! We want Philip!" Maybe it was the servants, whispering and giggling up a storm everywhere I looked. At the end of my leash, I pulled the footman up the stairs and down the long hall. But when I broke free and bounded eagerly into the suite, my little lady wasn't there! There was only one maid cleaning up. I ran around and sniffed, just to make sure my naughty girl wasn't hiding from me.

Where is she? Where is she?

The maid gave me a look of pure pity. "Poor thing. She wants her mistress. She's downstairs at her wedding breakfast, little luvie," she told me. "Did you see the cake, Nigel? It's nine feet high if it's an inch. I hear her ladyship and Prince Philip are going to cut it with his navy sword. What I wouldn't give to see that sight."

"I'd prefer the sight of a blazing hearth," Nigel said. He peeled off his coat and unclipped my leash and went off in search of warmth. I supervised the maid as she bustled about and made sure the royal apartment was spick-and-span.

We were just finishing up when Nigel returned wearing his coat and carrying my leash. Two outings in one afternoon! Could such a thing really be happening? This, indeed, was a special occasion. Nigel, I noted, looked less than enthusiastic. I daresay, the poor chap needed a heavier overcoat. Or a nice layer of fur. Or a double coat, such as I had. We headed back outside into the blowing sleet and went to stand by the side entrance. There we stood, in the thickening sleet. Nigel shivered while I looked eagerly about. My little lady would appear any moment, I just knew it.

And—what did I tell you?—the door swung open and there she was! I ran in circles and barked with delight.

"There you are, Susan!" she said, looking every bit as delighted to see me. "Are you ready to come with me on the royal honeymoon, you lucky little dog, you?"

I was glad to see that she was no longer wearing that frothy wedding gown. A lot of good it would do her in this sleet. She was now clad in a sensible suit and hat. Footmen assisted her into one side of the coach while long-legged Philip clambered into the other.

Somebody help me up, please, I barked. The seat of the royal coach was ever so much higher than a motorcar's. Far too high for my short legs to reach, no matter how hard I tried.

One of the eight horses pulling the coach turned and bobbed her head with its fancy plumed bridle. *Too bad you can't sprout wings and fly up there, eh, little nipper?*

Bow down a little lower, I snapped, *and I'll be happy to nip that feather off your head and make a set of wings with it.*

Lilibet patted the rug that covered her knees. "Come, Susan!"

"Up-sa-daisy!"

The page, bless the lad's heart, swooped down and lifted me. He delivered me into Lilibet's waiting arms. For one brief moment, our eyes locked. I knew then that nothing had changed. Married or not, she was still mine and I was still hers. Philip would just have to get used to the furry third party in this marriage.

She gently tucked me underneath the rug. It was deliciously warm in there, packed with hot water bottles to warm the royal knees. Of the thousands of cheering people who lined the streets that evening, not a one of them knew that hidden

beneath the lap blanket, all cozy and warm and loved, was Susan, the royal corgi.

At Waterloo Station, we were met by a band of photographers and reporters. Lilibet handed me off to Cyril, the footman. The flashbulbs blinded me, and I blinked. Reporters called out.

"Is the bride taking her dog on the honeymoon?" they shouted as they surged forward.

A band of bobbies kept the mob at bay while we made our way to the train platform.

In addition to myself and the newlyweds, our traveling party consisted of dear Bobo, Philip's valet, and a police detective who looked at me with narrowed eyes. A rather dodgy character, if you ask me. More flashbulbs exploded as we boarded the train and chugged away from the station in a cloud of steam.

I slept for the two-hour journey and woke up to discover that the sleet had turned to snow. Leaping up, I pressed my nose to the icy glass. I adore snow. I love to run through it. I love to eat it. I love to watch it fall. Have you ever noticed that everything smells different beneath a blanket of snow? Brighter, sharper, altogether more delicious.

When we arrived at the train station, a motorcar carried us to the estate of Philip's uncle Mountbatten. Lilibet and Philip and our party spent the first week of the honeymoon as his guests. I saw a good deal more of Cyril than I did of Lilibet. But the snow was a delightful distraction. One day, it fell so thickly, I ran up and down the garden paths, herding the big, furry white snowflakes like a flock of downy goslings.

A week later, our group moved on to more familiar territory: Balmoral, in Scotland. We stayed in one of the hunting lodges on the estate. It was a dark, musty place with heavy furnishings and enough tartan plaid to make me dizzy. But here the princesses had spent their summers in the simpler days before their father became king. This being one of Lilibet's favorite places on earth, it soon became mine, as well.

Lilibet and Philip and I settled in quite happily, and we spent many a contented hour in each other's company. There were no posh parties or dressing for dinner here. Balmoral wasn't that kind of place. There were quiet nights huddled before a roaring fire. There were days traipsing through the woods and over the moors. Don't tell the fashion-page editors, but Lilibet went around in adorably clunky army boots and a fleece-lined leather jacket. I often tagged along when she went with Philip on hunting expeditions.

Like many royals, they had a fondness for blood sports. I confess I felt sorry for the stags. Both Lilibet and Philip were deadeye shots, and those poor creatures never stood a chance.

Was it an honor to be felled by a royal bullet? I fancy not. Rather!

BABY CHARLES

Ever since the day reporters saw me in the royal carriage at Waterloo Station, the die was cast. I became very nearly as famous and sought after as the royal couple! The high fence surrounding Buckingham Palace kept me safe from prying eyes and nosy newspaper photographers eager to snap my photo. But reporters could still write whatever they pleased about me. Not that I could read it, but I'm sure they had their own bizarre ideas about what life was like for me behind royal doors. The Inside Scoop, as it were. I'd give them something to scoop.

But Lilibet ignored them all. As far as she was concerned, her corgi was nobody's business but her own.

The happy couple decided on St. James's Palace as their city residence. It was just down the Mall from Buckingham Palace. But the house was badly in need of repairs. So while it was being fixed up, they moved temporarily into an apartment in Buckingham Palace. The royal family called the palace the House. This was not meant nicely. None of them, not even the king and queen, cared for the House very much. They much preferred their residences in the country. But the House was their London headquarters and they were stuck with it, poor dears.

Calling Buckingham Palace a "house" is rather like calling me a teacup Chihuahua. It has 775 rooms, including 19 staterooms, 52 bedrooms, 188 bedrooms for staff, 92 offices, and 78 bathrooms. Whenever my lady was in the House, I stayed by her side. But when she and Philip were gone on one of their royal tours for the king, I ranged more widely. I pitter-pattered from room to room, sniffing and exploring, eager to find something to herd or chase. My tendency to wander in search of far-flung amusements rather vexed the staff.

"Come back here, Susan!" they would call out to me. But I kept on going with not so much as a by-your-leave. I was tame and obedient for no one but the princess. And I answered to no one but her.

Often on my palace rambles, I would leave a wee "contribution" on some elegant rug or drape. Was this shabby behavior? It was just my little way of showing that I was ruler of all I surveyed.

One time a new footman caught me at it. He grabbed me by the scruff and was fixing to rub my nose in my business. But a maid swooped down on him. "Oooh! Don't you dare, Danny!" she scolded. "No one can discipline Susan but the Royal Highness Princess Elizabeth herself! If she ever got wind of your doings, you'd lose your job, you would."

But did Lilibet ever scold me? Not once, that I can recall. I suppose you could say we had an understanding, she and I. We existed, together, in our own royal bubble. But one day, something happened to disturb the Bubble.

The first thing I noticed was that Her Royal Highness was not herself. Something was badly amiss. For one thing, she had lost the lovely roses in her cheeks and the sparkle in her eyes. Gone, too, was her healthy appetite. What little she did eat came up immediately after breakfast. I followed her into the loo and watched her with an anxious look.

"You're not to worry, Susan," she told me as she splashed her face with water. "I have a bit of morning sickness, that's all."

I whined, *Fix it!*

"The doctors say I shall be getting over it soon. This is what happens to some women when we are expecting."

In any event, her sickness in the mornings did not prevent her from having a jolly good time the rest of the day. She and Philip attended the horse races at Ascot together. They went to teas and parties and were often out dancing in nightclubs till all hours. And day by day, she grew more plump. The roses returned to her cheeks. Eventually, she was too plump to dance or go out in public. She was all mine then. It was just too, too delicious when she held me on her lap. But there was a warm lump in her tummy that grew bigger every day. When I put my ear to the lump, I thought I heard a steady *thumpety-thump* sound. Made my ears perk right up, I can tell you that. And then there were times when—egads!—the lump shifted and struck out, as if wanting to kick me off my little lady's lap!

Good sweet mother of all corgis! What was happening to my mistress?

That fall of 1948, a crew of men came to the palace and set to work with ladders and hammers and buckets of paint. In an attempt to keep them in an orderly herd, I chased after them, nipping at their heels. I ran myself ragged but, still, they insisted upon scattering their separate ways. And when the rooms were cleaned and painted, the men brought in strange new furniture and instruments.

I stood and watched, in a state of utter bafflement.

Sensing my mystification, Lilibet took me on a tour. "Instead of my going to a hospital, this is where I'm to have the baby," she explained to me.

Repairs and remodeling at the palace were nothing new to me. And whenever a given room was redone, I always made a point of passing through and leaving a modest contribution, just to mark my participation. But this suite smelled so clean, so new, so very important, that I couldn't bring myself to squirt so much as a single drop. Fancy that!

One night, following the evening meal, Lilibet clutched her tummy and said to Philip, "Darling, I think it's started."

My ears pricked.

So did Philip's. All of a sudden, he was a twitter of nerves as he rushed Lilibet to the new suite.

I trotted along behind them. All at once, Philip whirled upon me. In a sharp voice, he said, "Not you, Susan."

I stopped in my tracks and stared up at him. My eyes smoldered. *Very well, dear boy, if that's the way you want it. This time—and only this time—I'm willing to go along.* I watched as they disappeared from sight, giving the door a great big bang. Well, I never!

Moments later, strange-smelling men brushed past me and entered the room. Philip came out, and I followed him down to the palace gym. There, he commenced a round of squash. How bad could things be if he had time for sport? At sixes and sevens, I paced from room to room. The entire palace was ablaze with lights and abuzz with talk, both among the staff and the family. I looked from face to face, trying to understand what in the world was happening to my Lilibet.

Later that night, one of the staff announced that Princess Elizabeth had given birth to a seven-pound, six-ounce baby. A son.

Soon after, I heard him squalling.

A pup! So that was what the lump had been. My little lady was now a mother.

Later that night, the baby was carried into the ballroom for inspection. The staff stood and stared in awe. He was placed in a little cot and swaddled in white blankets. He was so very small, and he had such a very pink and wrinkly face. And he wriggled. But for all his tiny size, he had a very big name. They called him Charles Philip Arthur George. I say! Hip, hip, hooray and all that for the little baby with the long name.

"Imagine," one of the maids whispered to another, "one day that precious little bundle will be king of England."

The next time I saw Lilibet, she was in the royal apartment with that same precious bundle at her breast.

"I never thought one could be kept so busy in bed," she said to me with a contented sigh.

I kept my thoughts to myself. Philip I was

barely able to tolerate. But there was something about this defenseless little bundle that made me burn with jealousy.

Apparently, people outside the palace understood these feelings of mine. A newspaper called the *Daily Mirror* put out a request to its young readers to advise Lilibet on how to keep me, Susan, from growing jealous of the baby. One young man knew from his own experience of being a big brother. He wrote, "First. Show baby to Susan, stroking Susan all the time. Second. When nursing baby let Susan have a nice saucer of milk or tea beside you."

In the next weeks and months, I spent ever so much time being shown the wriggling bundle whilst being stroked and cooed at. And I drank enough milk to float one of Philip's navy vessels.

But never fear, boys and girls. In time, I grew to be almost as fond of the little prince as I was of his mother. How could I not? They had the same dark hair and bright eyes and the very same sweet scent. I was always on my best behavior around him. This turned out to be very good practice for me.

As it happened, my own experience of mother-hood lay just around the corner.

A Royal Litter!

It was some months later when I began to feel rather strangely myself. I felt restless and itchy and hot and hungrier than any ten corgis. I was also just a tad prickly. If another dog had come sniffing around me, I do believe I would have snapped his head clean off.

Leave it to my little lady to be the first to notice the change in me. We were at Balmoral. I had just polished off my breakfast, a special meat biscuit smothered in gravy made from Lilibet's secret recipe. Having licked my plate clean, I found myself still famished. I sat watching my lady's hand lift a scone to her lips. She eyed me, one eyebrow cocked.

"Still hungry, are we, Susan?" she asked.

Oh, yes, please, my eyes told her. *A bit of that deliciousness, if you please.*

She smiled, pinched me off a corner of her buttery scone, and tossed it to me.

No sooner had my jaws snapped and my throat swallowed than my eyes said, *More please? I'm ever so much hungrier than usual.*

"You know, darling," she said to Philip, "I think Susan may have just gone into heat."

"Has she really, now?" Philip said, with his nose in the newspaper. He could not have cared less. If I had burst into flames, I doubt he would have bothered to douse me with a cup of tea.

Lilibet gave me a look that was just between us gals. "Let's give you a little more time and see, shall we, dearest?"

As the days passed, my condition grew more dire. What was happening to me? I felt crazy and jumpy, and my bladder, never very dependable, was out of control. I kept the staff hopping. They followed along behind me with the blotting paper and the soda water, cleaning up messes as fast as I could make them.

And then, on a day when I thought it couldn't get any worse, I was leashed up and led away by a footman. It became immediately obvious that we weren't going to the garden. Where was he taking me? Had I made one mess too many? Eaten the princess out of palace and home? Was I such a pest that I was being banished from the royal presence?

"Up you go, girl."

The footman swept me in his arms and placed me in a motorcar. I sat on the seat and tried to console my fretful self with the scents blowing past the moving vehicle. At length, we came to a flat grassy area where an enormous metal object with birdlike wings rumbled.

"This is it, Susan," said the footman. "We're flying you south. By royal order of Princess Elizabeth."

He opened the door. When I failed to jump down with my usual eagerness, he picked me up and carried me into the belly of the big metal bird.

I sat in his lap as the bird rumbled and groaned and took off high into the air. At first, I was beside myself. My claws scrabbled at the window.

Let me out!

But the footman held me close and spoke to me gently, and eventually I calmed down. I pressed my nose to the glass.

Blimey, I said to myself. *Here I am, up with the blooming birds.*

At length, we landed with a bump. The hatch creaked open. The footman lifted me up and carried me outside. My nose twitched. We were in a new place. It smelled different—and yet somehow delightfully familiar.

We climbed into another motorcar. As the wind blew through the top of the window, I raised my nose and sniffed. I smelled heathland and honeysuckle. I smelled gorse and heather and the wavy hair grass of my distant youth. I heard the chirp of a wood lark and the melodic song of a warbler. I knew *exactly* where I was. In the place I was born: Surrey.

And so it came as no surprise when the automobile pulled up to Rozavel Kennels and my dear Thelma stepped out to greet me.

"Hello, Sue!" she said. "Welcome back! You're looking hale and hearty. And I've got just the mate for you! I hope you'll like him."

His name was Lucky Strike. He was a dashingly handsome Pembroke corgi, one of Thelma's champions. Thelma left the two of us alone to get acquainted.

You're a bit of a celebrity here at the kennel, Lucky Strike told me admiringly.

Is that so? I pretended not to know what he was talking about.

They say you're a princess who lives in a palace.

My mistress is the princess. I am merely her faithful companion, I said, with what I hoped was becoming modesty.

Said Lucky Strike, *I'm honored to meet you.*

Charmed, I'm sure, I replied.

With a sniff here and a sniff there, Lucky Strike and I struck up a beautiful friendship.

I stayed at the kennel. Like Lilibet, I soon grew plump and contented. Unlike her, however, I did not suffer the morning sickness. In fact, I was hungry and ate enough for three! Two months later, I gave birth to two lovely pups. Lilibet named them Sugar and Honey. What adorable little darlings they were! They were all head and clumsy paws. And I knew that, from then on, whenever Lilibet went away, I would always have company. In my private quarters at the kennel, I lay on my side while my puppies suckled.

Drink up and grow strong, my babies, I told them. *You have your father's powerful chest. And my fine ears. And only great things lie in store for you.*

They gazed up at me through pale, milky eyes.

We just want to snuggle here next to you, said Honey.

We love you so, dear Mummy, said Sugar.

The love I felt was quite unlike anything I'd ever experienced. Afterward, we would fall into a deep sleep, with me lying on my back and my babies draped over me.

When the pups were old enough to travel, we returned to the palace. Lilibet hovered over my basket and cooed at us.

Is she the One? Sugar asked.

Yes, I said. *I think you'll find that she possesses a gift for understanding corgis. In time, you will come to understand her.*

As my pups grew stronger, Lilibet was the only human I permitted to pick them up and stroke them.

I must say, it was a most satisfying experience, having a family of my own. After all, Lilibet was busy with her human family now. And while I did not know it at the time, her life was about to get *ever* so much busier.

A SAILOR'S WIFE

Not long after I whelped my puppies in 1949, we all moved into our redecorated quarters at St. James's Palace. My, but the staff had grown! All of Lilibet's former servants joined us there—including dearest Bobo. There was Philip's valet, a chef, and kitchen staff—plus a small army of butlers, footmen, and chauffeurs. Tiny Prince Charles even had his *own* staff: two Scottish nurses—a mean one named Helen and a gentler one called Mabel. He also had his own footman who served his meals and made sure the royal baby carriage was oiled and in fine working order. Imagine if you had a servant whose job it was to maintain your bicycle!

Philip very much wanted to continue his career in the navy. He had been attending school in the hopes that he might one day be captain of his own vessel. That fall, he was made second-in-command of one of His Majesty's ships. The only hitch? The ship's port was on the tiny island of Malta, in the Mediterranean Sea! When doctors informed Lilibet that it would not be safe to bring young Prince Charles to such a place, she decided to join her husband.

She left Prince Charles with me and the pups and the nurses at St. James's. This may seem odd to you. If your own parents went swanning off somewhere and left you with the servants, some might say they were being neglectful. But no one thought this about Lilibet and Philip. They were just behaving like royals. And if you haven't gathered this by now, the royals do things differently than the rest of us, don't they?

My pups and I loved being in the nursery, but only when Mabel was on duty. When Helen came on, we made ourselves scarce. The hatchet face on that one! It was enough to freeze the Welsh blood in our veins! I'm sure she was only safeguarding the royal tot. But I say, really now! Didn't she know that none of us would ever harm a hair on his dear little head? Hadn't I drummed that lesson into my pups' furry little heads from the moment they were weaned?

You mustn't ever hurt bonnie Prince Charles. Even if he tugs on your fur or pulls your tail, you're not to turn on him.

What about the other humans, Mum? Honey asked.

You must mind Lilibet and the king and queen—the princess's mum and dad—for they are your royal sovereigns. As for everyone else, if they bother you, issue a warning growl. If they persist, you have my permission to nip them. Try not to draw blood. Simply make clear that you are not to be trifled with. Sometimes it's the only way to get humans to behave.

That Christmas of '49, with Lilibet still away in Malta, I and my pups and Charles went to Sandringham to spend the holiday. Sandringham—yet another of the royal residences—was a big, drafty old pile in Norfolk. But we found ourselves surprisingly cozy there: Sugar and Honey and I, the little prince, the king, the queen, and a modest staff of over a hundred.

How the royal grandparents doted on Prince

Charles! I confess that I worried about the king. As happy as he was in the company of his grandchild, I sensed he was in great pain. He reeked of sickness. He had wasted away to a mere shadow of his former self.

What I gathered from the queen, who heard it from her daughter, was that Lilibet was having an absolutely smashing time on Malta. On that faraway island, she wasn't a princess. She was simply a sailor's wife. She could do whatever she wished and go wherever she wanted—with no nosy crowds or reporters or photographers pestering her. After five long weeks on Malta, my little lady returned at the end of the holiday. And, oh, how my corgi heart soared.

"Susan!" she told me as she held me and stroked my furry tummy. "I've been having such a good time. I drive myself all over the island. Imagine—

no chauffeur! I go out alone to get my hair done. Sometimes I shop with my girlfriends. And at night, Philip and I dine and go dancing. And the orange trees on that island! They smell simply heavenly."

I did not see very much of her during her all-too-brief stay. She was busy visiting with Prince Charles. And by March of 1950, she was gone again. This, as I had come to learn, was life with Lilibet. I was proving that even a dog can develop a Stiff Upper Lip. I tried to make the best of it. And, when the queen, who was just as fond of corgis as Lilibet, took Honey to live with her, I accepted that, too, with good grace.

When next Lilibet returned to us, in May, she was *that way* again. Yes, dear reader, she was *with child.* I knew the signs. The pale cheek. The bulge in her tummy. The morning sickness. Fortunately, the little prince was too busy toddling about to sit on his mother's gradually shrinking lap. Once again, I enjoyed that privilege. Late that summer, Lilibet gave birth to a female pup: Anne Elizabeth Alice Louise.

Shortly after Charles's second birthday, in November of that same year, Lilibet again left for Malta. And we spent a second Christmas at Sandringham. Being reunited with Honey was great fun. The three of us tore around the halls of the

castle until we were quite tuckered out. Then we lay down and caught our breath before leaping up and tearing around some more. Every so often, one of us would leave a little squirt at the base of the Christmas tree. After all, what are trees for? Jolly good fun!

As we sat around the tree one night, catching our breath, the queen read a letter. I could sense that it had come from Lilibet because the writing paper smelled of her special sweetness. The queen folded it up with a smile on her face.

"You know," she said to the king, "I think our daughter likes being the wife of a common sailor. She and Philip are having the time of their lives."

"That will all stop when she comes to the throne," the king said glumly.

"I think Lilibet has the gift of being able to enjoy herself whatever the circumstances."

If the king was gloomy, it was only because he felt so ill. He had a terrible cough, and the hand he reached out to pet me with often burned with fever. How he worried me, the poor man!

I believe it was the king's declining health that finally brought Elizabeth back to the fold. She arrived just in time to stand in for her father at a parade of the British Royal Army on palace grounds. It was a ceremony steeped in tradition called the Trooping of the Color.

From a window of Buckingham Palace, we all looked down upon the parade grounds, where Lilibet sat upon a big brown horse. She wore a tunic like the soldiers and a cap with a long white plume. I fretted, as did her mum. Lilibet always sat astride her horse, just like a man. But today she rode sidesaddle, like a lady, with both legs slung off to one side. It was probably all in the name of tradition.

But what good was tradition if you fell off a horse? Still, she rode with grace and confidence at the head of a long parade of stiff and sober-looking soldiers.

We watched as she drew to a halt, back straight and chin high. In her left hand, she clasped the reins and her crop. With her right hand, she saluted the men as they filed past her for inspection. We

were all bursting with pride for our Lilibet.

But the absolute highlight of the day was when his great-uncle Mountbatten boosted the young prince Charles in his arms so his mum could look up and see him at the window. The wee lad lifted his chubby little hand and saluted her.

I say! Ripping good show!

Her Royal Majesty

It was February 1952, and my little lady and Philip had just left for another tour in the name of the king. This time, they were off to Africa. Sugar and I were at Sandringham with the grandparents the king and queen, the little prince and princess, and, of course, my Honey.

Our host, His Royal Majesty King George VI, was in excellent spirits. He went out to pursue what had always been, since he was a lad, his favorite blood sport—shooting rabbits.

He must have had a wonderful time because that evening, when he went to bed, he swore to his servant that he would get up tomorrow and go out shooting more rabbits.

I knew the moment I awoke the next morning that something was wildly amiss. Ears perked, I listened. I heard the servants tiptoeing about. I rose from my bed and prowled around, the pups at my heels. Nothing was as it should have been. Servants went about drawing drapes and covering mirrors in black cloth. They spoke in grave whispers. My nostrils twitched. The house smelled different.

It was the smell of death.

What's happening, Mum? Sugar asked fearfully.

The king is dead, I said in reply. *There will*

be no more rabbit shooting for His Majesty.

Sugar sniffed. *I suppose the rabbits will be happy.*

Honey let out a forlorn little sigh. *But all the rest of us will be very sad. He was always so good to us.*

Poor Lilibet! Sugar burst out. *She has lost her dear papa!*

She will be quite undone when she finds out, I said.

What will happen now? Honey asked.

She will no longer be a sailor's wife. My little lady will be queen of England.

What does that make us? Sugar asked.

Why, the queen's corgis, of course, said I.

When Lilibet arrived at Sandringham, she looked pale and so very sad. She greeted her sister, Margaret Rose, and her mum, the king's widow. Her mother's eyes brimmed with tears. She wept, not just over the loss of her husband but also for her daughter Elizabeth, who was frightfully young for a queen. Lilibet was just about to bid farewell to her father's body, when she noticed me. I was standing faithfully nearby, expecting nothing, ready to give my all if called upon.

"Susan!" she cried, and swept me up in her arms. I expected her to weep into my ruff. Instead, she murmured, "How I've missed you! You should have been there with us in Kenya, my darling. We were staying in a hotel built into a giant fig tree. From its branches, we looked down into the bush upon all sorts of wild animals: rhinos and monkeys and elands and impalas. You would have been quite beside yourself. Then I saw a herd of elephants. They were pink, Susan! Imagine you, herding a pack of pink elephants. And then someone told me that they weren't pink at all. They had merely been rolling in some pink-colored dust. But I like to think that I saw pink elephants. Oh, Susan, my dear!" She sighed. "How dreadful this all is! Everything will be different now. But I must step up and do the best job I can."

Later, I overheard one of the maids say that Lilibet was now the fortieth monarch to sit on the English throne since William the Conqueror. When she emerged from the royal bedchamber, the servants all bowed and curtsied before her. They looked at her differently now. She was no longer the king's daughter, a carefree child of the household. She was a brave young woman taking on a very serious job. The other royals even treated her differently. She (and I) now entered every room first, followed by Philip and then everyone else. And from that day on, dear boys and girls, she ceased to be Lilibet to me and became Elizabeth, Her Royal Highness.

We moved back to Buckingham Palace: Philip and Elizabeth, Charles and Anne, the servants and myself and Sugar. My little lady did not have the crown yet. But with or without a crown, she behaved like a queen and got right down to business. As did we dogs.

Under this new arrangement, Sugar and I—and Honey, when the Queen Mum was in residence, which was often—were given our own quarters. It was a room down the hall from Elizabeth's, right next to the page's pantry. As it happened, this was all the Queen Mum's idea. Her thought was that dogs living in a palace were royalty. Three cheers for the Queen Mum!

Every day, the bell rang to signal that it was

mealtime. A page put out a plastic sheet over the carpet outside Elizabeth's sitting room. He set out silver bowls with our names engraved on them. It took seven people to feed us.

The Palace Clerk typed up the day's menu and posted it on the kitchen wall. The menu changed daily. My lady consulted on every detail. We never ate food from a can or a bag. We ate steak and rice, poached chicken, and braised liver. When we were at Windsor or Sandringham or one of the other country residences, we ate game—mostly rabbit from which the bones had been removed. We never, ever ate the same thing two days in a row. Elizabeth simply would not stand for it. One time she heard a rumor that someone had served us meat that had been thawed from the deep freeze. She had a stern word in the kitchen over that little bit of carelessness, I can tell you! It was fresh food only for us.

Down in the kitchen, the Royal Chef supervised the preparation of each meal. His assistant carried it to the door. He was met there by a footman, who bore the tray upstairs and over to the corridor outside the sitting room. Then the page took the tray from the footman and filled the bowls on the mat. Sometimes, Elizabeth did the honors. When the weather was fair, we ate outside on the terrace overlooking the gardens.

Immediately following every meal, we went out for Walkies in the garden. When we came back inside, we waited impatiently while the footman dried off our paws with a towel. And then we would drag him back upstairs to the royal apartment to see Her Highness.

We usually arrived just as Bobo did with Elizabeth's tea tray. We burst in the door behind her, nearly toppling the old girl, and dashed over to greet our adored mistress.

Elizabeth kept a special stool by her bed just for us. We leapt up onto the stool and from there onto the bed, where we gave her good-morning kisses.

"Hello, my darlings!" she said, holding us in her arms, wreathed in corgi fur.

No matter how busy her day, Elizabeth always had time to snuggle with us.

We lolled about while she took her bath, which Bobo drew for her at just the right temperature, not too hot and not too cold. Afterward, Bobo helped her dress and did her hair. Then Elizabeth did *our* hair—or, rather, our fur—giving us each a good brisk brushing. While she groomed us, she often listened to a small portable radio, on which a man with a deep voice spoke of vastly important matters. Elizabeth never wanted to be out of touch with what was happening outside the palace. She carried the radio with her into the private dining room, where breakfast awaited. She liked a boiled egg or toast with a pat of butter from the royal dairy. We watched her eagerly, and she never failed to toss us a bit of buttery toast. She always aimed for me first, then the pups. Age, as I was coming to know—just like royalty—has its privileges.

While she nibbled on toast and sipped Earl Grey tea, she would scan the newspapers, always reading the sports papers first, keeping up with the horse racing news. We were just finishing breakfast when that horrible noise started. It happened every day at exactly the same time, but we never got used to it. We leapt up and ran to the window and complained bitterly.

Down below, a man in a swinging plaid skirt blew into a vile instrument called the bagpipe.

Why, oh why, must we listen to this every day? yowled Sugar.

Why must he play so loudly? howled Honey.

Elizabeth's great-great-grandmother Queen Victoria started the tradition, I explained to them. *And, as you know, the royals are* all about *tradition.*

This is one tradition I wish they would do away with, Sugar moaned.

If I ever get my paws on that bagpipe, Honey groaned, *I'll rip it to pieces, I will.*

Now, now, children. Stiff Upper Lip, I reminded them.

I was scarcely able to tolerate the noise myself. Elizabeth, on the other paw, seemed to thrive on the racket. She insisted that every day start this way. Perhaps, like a cold shower, it woke her up and readied her for what was to come.

After the din subsided, Elizabeth sat down at her desk and got to work. We corgis lay on the floor, in classic corgi style, on our bellies with our legs splayed out in what is known as the flying squirrel formation. While we napped, she would answer her correspondence or confer with her private secretaries. They arrived daily bearing baskets full of papers that needed signing and two boxes covered in red leather. She opened the red leather boxes with a special key. What did the boxes contain? Secret papers would be my guess. But then again, dogs cannot read, so everything humans write is a secret to us.

After lunch, if she had no appointments, Elizabeth would take us for a long walk in the palace gardens. And, oh, how pleasurable it was!

The pages or footmen who sometimes walked us were often impatient, urging us through our rounds at a brisk pace. Had Elizabeth known this, she would have been most displeased. When she did the honors, Her Royal Majesty took her time. She had a deep appreciation for the moments that are important to a dog. Watching the leaves drift to the ground. Sniffing a scent. Herding a swarm of

butterflies. Squatting to do our business in just the right spot. I believe she cherished these walks with us. Why? Because when she was with us, she wasn't a queen. Everyone else scraped and bowed before her. But to us, she was simply our dear little lady, the one who kissed us and groomed us and fed us and took us for Walkies.

In the afternoons, while Elizabeth entertained visitors or had her hair washed and set, we dogs alternately ran around and curled up and napped. We woke from our afternoon nap when the page came through the door, wheeling the lace-draped tea cart with its delectable cargo of tiny sandwiches and scones and gingerbread and muffins. Believe me, dear boys and girls, you haven't lived until you've had high tea at Buckingham Palace!

We gathered around the table and eagerly waited for the bits of scone and gingerbread Elizabeth tossed down to us. When the children had tea with their mum, we got the additional delicious bits and bobs that fell from their hands. Sometimes, we even licked their sticky fingers and faces. By the time the nanny came and bore them off for bedtime, we had eaten just enough to tide us over until dinner.

When Prince Philip dined with the queen, we were often banished to our quarters. I tried to be sporting about it. After all, we'd enjoyed her company for most of the day. The prince was not my favorite person in the world, but he deserved his time alone with Elizabeth.

Our days passed in a delightful whirl of pampered routine. And then one day I began to hear a new word around the palace. The air rang with it. The word was *coronation*. I had never heard it before, and I had no idea what it meant. But this much I can tell you. It wreaked havoc on our daily schedule.

CROWNS AND CLOCKS

This coronation business was the highlight of Elizabeth's life. Yes, outshining even her eighteenth birthday, when she received yours truly as a gift. It required endless discussions and preparation. I have met dogs, at Sandringham and Balmoral, who have been bred and trained to compete in rather posh affairs called dog shows. This coronation, it seemed to me, was exactly like a dog show for royalty. And make no mistake: Elizabeth was going for Best in Show. And the preparation and practice threw our daily routine into chaos, I tell you!

A stuffy little man they called the archbishop came to visit early almost every morning. He sat in the sitting room and slurped tea and droned on while Elizabeth cocked her head and listened.

Later in the morning, down in the ballroom, she practiced for the coronation ceremony. A bossy man called the Duke of Norfolk directed her to walk about with sheets tied to her shoulders onto which weights had been sewn. The sheets were frightful heavy, but she always moved with stately ease and grace. Never once did my little lady stumble or falter.

Afternoons, she sat at her desk answering letters or reading the secret papers from the red box. Perched on her head was an enormous object that sparkled with jewels.

I stared up at her in puzzlement. She looked down at me and smiled.

"It's a crown, Susan. This particular crown is known as the St. Edward's Crown. It was used in the coronation of Charles II, in 1651. I shall be wearing it during the coronation ceremony. It weighs five pounds, so I must get used to its weight, just as I must get used to my duties as queen. The crown is the single most important symbol of the British monarchy."

I licked my lips and growled. For a symbol, it looked frightfully heavy. Perhaps she would need my help carrying it? As usual, my little lady read my mind.

"Sorry, darling. The ceremony's to be held at Westminster Abbey."

Westminster Abbey? Wasn't that where she had taken her wedding vows? Apparently, no one had seen fit to change the rules. There were still no dogs allowed. The very idea!

One day in the ballroom, instead of sheets she wore a fur-trimmed cloak with a long train that took six ladies-in-waiting to carry. Wearing the heavy crown and dragging the cloak, she walked around and around. She did this endlessly. Then the duke finally asked, "Would Your Majesty care to rest?"

She said, "I'll be all right. I'm as strong as a horse."

When I heard the dreaded word *horse,* I gaped. Now *horses* were being brought into this? It wasn't bad enough that my lady had to be burdened with a crown and a cape? Would she also have to perch on a horse in the treacherous sidesaddle position? Did they even *let* horses into the abbey? And if so, why weren't corgis allowed, too? This was an outrage! A scandal, I tell you.

On a bonnie day in June, I stood by and watched as Bobo and the other maids helped Elizabeth into her fancy gown. It was a lovely garment: white silk embroidered with strange symbols.

Pointing to them, Elizabeth said to her ladies, "These are the emblems of all the nations belonging to our vast empire. The rose of England, the thistle of Scotland, the leek of Wales, the shamrock of Ireland, the oak leaf of Canada, the lotus flowers of India and Ceylon, the wheat shaft of Pakistan, and so on."

She showed them a small picture in the exact spot where her hand naturally rested.

"And that is a four-leaf clover . . . for good luck," she said.

An Irish setter once told me that a four-leaf clover meant something magical to humans. Perhaps queens needed a bit of magic to rule their kingdoms. Perhaps my corgi enchantment would come in handy now.

After one quick kiss on my nose, she was gone in a flurry of rustling silk.

The pups and I retired to the Corgi Room to have a little lie-down. The disruption of our routine over the past weeks had been exhausting.

Suddenly, I heard noises nearby. I sat up and panted. They were coming from the room next door. The three of us hopped out of our beds and sallied forth. A crowd had gathered in the pantry. They stood staring at a noisy little box sitting on the counter.

What are they doing? Sugar asked.

What is that noisy little box they're all staring at? Honey wanted to know.

It is a magic box, I said, *that allows the staff to see the goings-on in Westminster Abbey.*

I want to see, too! Sugar and Honey demanded, tails awag.

I led them, nosing our way through the forest of legs, until we were standing in front of the magic box.

One of the footmen said, "I hear the ceremony

is being broadcast on televisions clear around the world."

We peered up at the box—this contraption the footman called a television. In it, I saw masses of people lining the streets of London standing in torrents of rain—your typical English weather—watching a parade. The people seemed happy and excited as they cheered the parade. Music poured out of the television. It was the music of the bands marching in the parade. And—egads!—there were bagpipers, too! Thankfully, the sound was muffled.

Someone said, "There are twenty-nine bands and twenty-seven carriages in the parade."

One of the maids added, "And soldiers from fifty different nations. It's so exciting!"

In a large carriage, a big smiling woman waved to the cheering crowds. She wore a regal robe. On her head sat a crown with a long feather in it.

"Whoever is that?" one of the pages asked.

"The reporter said it's the queen of Tonga. Doesn't she look splendid?"

The picture changed, showing a huge building with tall spires.

"Westminster Abbey," someone said in a voice of awe.

A fairy-tale carriage pulled by four teams of gray horses drew to a halt before it. I sat down hard and growled. Those horses had better not be entering the abbey!

"That's her!" said the maid. "That's Her Royal Majesty! Doesn't she look fetching?"

As my lady stepped out of the carriage, her head was bare, and she looked small and cold in her white dress. She slipped into the church. I yawned and licked my lips. I know you'll think me terrible, but I stretched out and fell asleep. I simply couldn't keep my eyes open a moment longer. I felt wrung out from the excitement of the past few weeks. And when I woke up, everyone in the room and on the television was clapping and cheering. Queen Elizabeth II was coming out of the church in her crown and long cape.

All that fuss and worry and it was over during the time it took me to take the merest wink of a nap.

In the months after the coronation, Elizabeth and Philip traveled the kingdom far and wide. The following June, in 1954, Sugar and Honey and I were at Windsor Castle, keeping company with Prince Charles and Princess Anne.

The children were in bed, fast asleep. We corgis were dozing on the carpet, when, suddenly, I beheld a man stealing into the room.

Sugar, who had always been a heavy sleeper, snoozed on. But Honey's head snapped up. *Who goes there?*

Hush, child. Let Mummy take care of this.

My hackles rose. I growled deep in my throat. I flew at him and clamped my jaw around his leg.

"Help!" he screamed.

Honey started barking, cheering me on, and Sugar woke up and joined in.

Miss Lightbody, the new nanny, came running. She threw up her arms and shook her fists and said very sternly, "Susan—NO! NO! Bad, BAD girl! Down."

I held on to the man's leg and growled at her. *Try and make me. I answer only to the queen.*

She got down on her knee and said to me in a much gentler voice, "Susan, dear, he's a friend. Not a foe. Let him loose immediately, please."

116

Firmly, she grabbed my collar in one hand and the man's leg in the other, and managed to pry us apart. She was stronger than she looked.

"I'm so very sorry," she said to the man.

To me she said, "Don't you recognize Mr. Hubbard? He is the Royal Clock Winder!"

I growled. Of course I recognized him. He was the man who kept the nursery clock in the big box ticking night and day. For the past few days, that thing had gone blessedly silent, and I liked it that way. What use has a dog for a clock? My nose is all the clock I need. My thinking was that, with a little nipping, I could convince the man never to wind that clock again.

I broke loose from Miss Lightbody and once again went for him.

But the man shook me off, and drat! He opened the cabinet and began to wind that clock!

By now, the children were awake and other servants had arrived. Before the scene grew any uglier, I stood down. I knew when I had lost. Seething, I watched Mr. Hubbard as he finished winding the clock.

Tick-tick-tick-tick. For the rest of that night, I lay on the rug and sulked. I closed my eyes and heard the clock *tick-tick-ticking* as, in my dreams, I ran in hot pursuit of the dreaded Royal Clock Winder.

Now that Elizabeth was on the throne, the press

was eager for new stories. They pounced upon this one. There must have been spies in the household. The next day, the newspaper headlines screamed: QUEEN'S CORGI LOSES MIND AND ATTACKS ROYAL WINDER!

Such balderdash! Was no one in England interested in reading the truth? Not a single reporter asked me for my side of the story.

On the day she returned, the queen whispered in my ear, "I hear you've been very busy while I was away. Guarding the nursery from the wicked Clock Winder. You never did like that clock, did you? Well, I don't blame you one bit. I don't, either."

It was so good to know that Her Majesty was still on my side.

10

MY TIME COMES

Toward the end of the same year I gave what-for
to the Royal Clock Winder, I also became a proud
grandmum. Sugar was sent to Rozavel to be mated
with a handsome Pem corgi by the name of Rebel-
lion. She returned to us in due course, with the
grandpups, Whiskey and Sherry. Her Royal Highness was meant to choose one of the pups to keep.
She sent for Prince Charles and Princess Anne to
help her make the decision.

"Oh, please take the one with the white on his chest!" Anne begged.

"I prefer the one with the big, floppy feet," Charles said.

White on chest or floppy feet? Elizabeth simply could not make up her mind. The fact is, she wanted *both* pups. And she was queen now, so who was to say she couldn't have both?

She drew her children close to her and whispered, "Don't tell your father. But we've got *two new puppies*! One for each of you. Just in time for Christmas!"

"Really?" said Prince Charles. "I'll take Whiskey."

"And may I have Sherry?" asked Anne.

"Yes, yes, of course, my darlings!"

But both Elizabeth and I knew the truth, and I'll let you in on it if you promise not to tell. *All* us corgis *really* belonged to her. And now there were five of us in the palace. Not long after that, Honey had pups of her own—Bee and Buzz. And then there were seven.

We were fast outnumbering the royal family!

The page whose job it was to take us out for Walkies now had more leashes than he knew what to do with! Perhaps that was why I was allowed to run freely in the garden. Not that I was doing much running these days. Truth to tell, I was getting on in years.

Why can't we go off the leash, too? Whiskey whined.

Because you're a silly little pup, said Honey, *who can't be trusted.*

Besides, said Sugar, *Susan is the mother of us all. That gives her special privileges.*

It was a typical London day. A deliciously milky mist hung over the gardens, allowing me to dig up a bed of fragrant jasmine without any of the gardeners seeing. Through the fog, I heard the page wrestling with leashes. The more those naughty little corgis ran around him, the more bollixed up he became.

I was just standing over the hole I had dug and sneezing the dirt from my nose, when I saw a strange dog appear out of the mist. Who was this shaggy man of mystery?

When in doubt, growl. *Who let* you *in?* I asked. There was a high iron fence surrounding palace grounds and guards everywhere you looked.

He sniffed as he made his way over to me. He looked a bit dodgy. Scruffy he was, with a ragged ear and scars crisscrossing his hide.

Cor blimey, while you was digging in that there hole, I thought you was a big dog, but you're just a wee slip of a gal, ain't you, with them short little legs!

That got my hackles up. *Watch your tongue! I'm big enough to handle the likes of you,* I told him.

Now calm yourself, miss. No offense intended, I'm sure. To answer your question, I let myself in by digging me a hole underneath the fence, he said. *We street dogs is clever that way.*

If they catch you, they'll toss you out on your ragged ear, I told him. *Or worse. Why take the risk?*

Call it curiosity. I pass by this garden every day and gets me a snootful of dog. But I says to myself, "Self, ain't no dog could possibly be allowed in there."

Oh, but we are. We're the queen's corgis, I said proudly. *And this is our domain.*

So it's all true, he said. *The word on the street is that the dogs who live here are treated like royalty.*

Pishposh, I said. *It's a simple enough life that we lead.*

You don't say? Well, let me tell you about my *sim-*

ple life. Me and my mates, we sleep in alleyways and scratch our fleas till our flesh is right raw. We wake up every morning and go rooting through dustbins for scraps of food. Shopkeepers dump cold water on us. Little ones throw rocks at us. And nobody, but nobody, ever touches us or feeds us or so much as calls us friend.

I was shocked. That a member of *our* noble species, in this day and age and in one of the greatest cities on earth, should be living in such a state of neglect and poverty. It made my blood boil.

Say, love, tell me about this simple life of yours, the street dog said.

And so I told him. I told him about the raised wicker beds and the silver engraved feed dishes. I told him about the seven servants who prepared and served us our meals of liver and steak and tender rabbit—always fresh and never the same menu two days in a row. I told him about Walkies with

the queen and high tea at Buckingham Palace.
When I was finished, my visitor stared at me with
his eyes wide and his jaw hanging.

Blimey! he said at last. *You dogs have got it better
than a good many humans—let alone dogs.*

I brooded for a bit. For the first time, I found
myself feeling slightly ashamed of my good for-
tune.

The street dog nodded and said, *Let me tell you
one thing, miss. You'd never last a day out on the street.*

I should think not, I said with a shiver.

A crafty look came over my friend's furry face.
*Say, you don't suppose I can interest Her Royal High-
ness in taking in a new dog?*

I'm afraid not, I said kindly. *The queen only has
corgis, and you don't look as if you have much corgi
in you.*

Ain't that the truth? he said. *Well, I better be*

moseying along before that there fellow untangles himself and comes after me with a net.

I'm sorry you can't stay. I had actually enjoyed our little chin-wag. It was fascinating to hear about the World Out There. *My name is Susan, by the way. And yours is . . . ?*

I don't know as I have a name, he said as he scratched at a flea.

Fancy that! A dog who had nothing, not even a name to call his own. *Do you mind if I give you one?* I asked.

Suit yourself, miss, he said. *Call me anything you like, but whatever you do, don't call the dog warden.* He chuckled.

I think I'll call you Scrappy. Because you must fight valiantly for every scrap you get.

Scrappy it is, then. But don't you go feeling sorry for me, miss, he said. *I don't mind me life one jot. It might be hard. But I figure at least I have me freedom. Can you say the same?*

If freedom meant being flea-bitten and digging around in the trash for dinner, I wanted no part of it. But I didn't say so to him. I merely wished my friend Scrappy good luck and dogspeed.

And from that day forth, whenever I caught one of the little ones complaining, I would trot out the Tale of Scrappy and say, *Thank your lucky stars you were born into a royal household and not into some dark alley behind the dustbins.*

As the days flew by in a blur for my busy queen, they began to slow down for me. I was no longer a young pup. Her Royal Highness took excellent care of me, as always. When my joints grew stiff, she fed me fish oil and gave me a boost up onto the couch. When my teeth loosened, she made sure the chef mashed up my food. She still remembered to include me in her royal activities whenever possible. I flew with her by plane or whirlybird when she went to the country residences. Those times she entertained important visitors, like presidents and movie stars and royalty from across the sea, I was there at her side.

"What a cute little dog," the visitors would coo as they bent down to pet me.

And, no matter how important they were, Elizabeth would say, "Please don't pet the corgis." That was a privilege reserved for Her Royal Highness only.

When my time came to cross into the Great Hereafter, we were at Sandringham. As my vision dimmed, her dear face was the last sight I saw. Did she shed a tear for me? It may have been that a few tears fell on that Stiff Upper Lip of hers. She would miss me—that much I knew—because after my passing, she wrote a letter to the estate manager. There was a pet cemetery on the grounds started by

Elizabeth's great-great-grandmum Queen Victoria. Elizabeth drew a sketch of my gravestone and the words she wished to have engraved upon it.

SUSAN

DIED 26TH JAN 1959

FOR 15 YEARS THE FAITHFUL COMPANION OF THE QUEEN

Faithful companion. Very prettily put.

Later, she wrote another letter to the manager and asked him to insert my birthday, 20th Feb 1944, and to change the last line to read "For *almost* 15 years the faithful companion of the Queen."

That was my little lady for you: big of heart and, at the end of the day, a stickler for getting things correct.

At the end of her days, Her Royal Majesty

surely will leave behind a noble legacy of speeches and deeds and royal descendants. As for me, Hickathrift Pippa—also known as Susan—I left a legacy of my own. I was the founding mum of a formidable corgi dynasty. And what was my reward for this excellent work? In the afterlife, I was allowed to return to the fairy realm, where, to this very day, I proudly pull the carriage of the queen of the fairies herself.

Do you doubt my words? Allow me to suggest, boys and girls, the next time you are lucky enough to meet up with a corgi: take a closer look. I am quite sure that you will see in the rich red depths of his or her fur the very faintest tracings of a fairy saddle and harness. And if you are even luckier, you might, like my dearest Lilibet, find yourself touched by corgi enchantment.

APPENDIX

The Queen's Corgis

King Henry XIII had his hunting hounds. King Charles II had the Cavalier spaniels that now bear his name. Queen Victoria had her collies. But no British monarch has been more strongly identified with a single breed of dog than Queen Elizabeth II is with corgis.

Princess Diana, her late daughter-in-law, called them the "moving carpet" that was forever at her feet. Long-suffering Prince Philip once said, "Why do there have to be *so many?*" Palace gardeners despair of them digging up flower beds. Housekeepers complain of them soiling priceless carpets, drapes, and antiques. One member of the palace staff, under condition of anonymity, said, "They are yappy, snappy ankle biters, and the queen refuses to housebreak them."

Queen Elizabeth had corgis for pets almost all her life, from the time she was seven. Her first, Dookie, was a gift from her father. Willow, among her very last, helped his mistress celebrate her ninetieth birthday. Susan, aka Hickathrift Pippa, was a present from her parents on Elizabeth's eighteenth birthday. Susan remained at Elizabeth's side through her marriage to Prince Philip, her coronation, the birth of her children, and the first six years of her historic reign. The more than thirty corgis that followed were all descended from Susan.

At first, Rozavel's owner and manager, Thelma Gray, oversaw the breeding of the royal corgis. But within ten years, Elizabeth herself took on the task, with the resulting pups being registered under the title of Windsor Kennels. This venture resulted in the purest line of corgis ever bred, amounting to some fourteen generations—all descended from a single mother: Susan.

The queen is single-handedly responsible for starting a veritable corgi craze. And, like the queen, people admire the dogs' smarts, athleticism, and loyalty. Short in the leg, they are big on personality and an inspiration to artists and designers around the world. A corgi named Ein is the star of a popular Japanese anime series. Corgi imagery appears on socks, T-shirts, pillows, pajamas, fabric, jewelry, wallpaper, gift wrap, coffee cups, greeting cards—you name the product line, there's probably a corgi-themed version of it on the market or in the works. In fact, the corgi is fast becoming a popular tattoo design! This once rough-and-ready working dog from the farms of Wales has become a symbol of refinement, friendliness, and goodwill.

And can the dorgi be far behind? Yes, the queen has also popularized the crossbreed known as the dorgi—a corgi-dachshund mix—when she mated one of her corgis with Pipkin, her sister Princess Margaret Rose's beloved dachshund.

Her Royal Majesty's fondness for corgis is known throughout the world. When she and Prince Philip visited Grand Cayman in 1983, for instance, they were presented with a striking black coral statue of a corgi. The Buckingham Palace gift shop is piled high with stuffed corgis. And corgis appear in many royal portraits of the queen.

In 2012, when London hosted the Summer Olympics, the royal corgis were featured on international television when the actor Daniel Craig, famous for portraying James Bond, went to Buckingham Palace to escort the queen to the opening ceremony. The camera followed Mr. Craig as he strode down the halls of the palace with a furry corgi convoy at his heels.

Queen Elizabeth is not the only corgi lover in the royal family. The Queen Mother also fancied the breed. A bronze statue on the Mall in London shows "the Queen Mum" with two faithful corgis nearby in bas-relief. It was she who started the tradition of treating corgis like royalty, giving them elevated wicker beds, engraved silver food dishes, and custom-prepared meals fit, if not for a king, then certainly for a royal corgi. Princess Margaret, having grown up with corgis, also owned many in her adult life, all gifts from her sister. The grown-up Prince Charles, however, seems to have transferred his favor from corgis to Jack Russells.

In spite of the corgis' pampered existence (or perhaps because of it), the queen's dogs have not always displayed model canine behavior. For one thing, they are only partially housebroken, and that, apparently, is the way the queen likes it! A large supply of soda water and blotting paper is kept on hand at all times, and footmen diligently follow after the corgis, who are, by and large, given the run of the palace. The royal corgis have, at various times over the past few decades, bitten not only the royal clock winder but also the royal chauffeur, a palace guard, a soldier, a policeman, a postman, and who knows how many members of the palace staff who aren't telling. Perhaps understandably, there is said to be some resentment among the servants toward these pups.

So who disciplines these dogs? When it comes to naughty corgis, the queen is the only one allowed, and she is far from strict. Why this is so, one can only wonder. Has she been too often absent and unable to reinforce training? Is she too busy with affairs of state? Or is she simply softhearted? One explanation might be this: that she herself was born into captivity in her role as queen. Her life consists of an endless procession of rituals, obligations, and duties that she must never shirk. Year after year, she is required to smile and wave, make polite conversation with strangers from around the world, and, above all else, uphold tradition. Is it any wonder that she enjoys having a pack of corgis of which very little is asked—except to love her as much as she loves them—and who are, perhaps, just a little bit wild?

After seven decades, the corgi dynasty has had its day. In 2015, the queen announced that she would breed no more corgis. The line that started with Susan would now end. But this decision hasn't prevented Her Majesty from adopting.

Whisper was the beloved pet of one of her game-keepers. When the man passed away in 2017, the queen began taking Whisper for walks—and fell in love with him.

Long live the queen! Long live her corgis!

You can read more on the queen's corgis here:

- vanityfair.com/style/2016/05/queen-elizabeth -corgis

The Dwarf Dog

The word *corgi* is said to come from the Welsh words *cor* and *gi,* meaning "dwarf dog." There are two kinds of corgis: Pembroke and Cardigan. Both have short legs, long bodies, and foxy faces. But since 1934, both the British and the American Kennel Clubs have designated them as separate breeds. The Pembroke has a shorter body and toes that turn in. It has a naturally short tail, or else it is surgically shortened, or docked, at between two and five days old. Pems are part of the spitz family of dogs, which includes Pomeranians, Samoyeds, and chow chows. The Cardigan, with a longer body, toes that turn out, and a full tail, shares more traits with the dachshund and the basset. Of the two corgi breeds, the Pembroke is thought to be friendlier and more affectionate and, perhaps because of this, is the more popular breed, usually ranked in the top twenty on the American Kennel Club (AKC) list.

Historians say the Welsh corgi dates back to the twelfth century, when Henry I of England invited Flemish weavers to settle in Wales. They brought their dogs to herd the sheep that provided their wool. Welsh farmers came to use these dogs to herd cattle in the fields and geese and chickens to the marketplace. A noisier or more raucous breed of dog might have scattered the skittish fowl, but corgis—intent and relatively quiet—were perfect for the job.

It wasn't until the 1900s that the world outside of Wales began to pay much attention to corgis. But thanks to the efforts of breeders like Thelma Gray and Queen Elizabeth, corgis moved up from fields and farms to yards and houses—and even to castles and palaces!

For more about corgis, visit the AKC website:

• akc.org/dog-breeds/pembroke-welsh-corgi

Owning a Corgi

The Pembroke Welsh corgi is a long, strong, sturdy dog set close to the ground. For good reason, it is often called a "big dog on short legs." It measures ten to twelve inches at the shoulder and weighs up to thirty pounds. Its head looks quite foxy with a sharp muzzle and pointed, widely spaced ears. Its short, thick, weather-resistant coat ranges in color from red to faun to black and tan with white markings in the neck, head, muzzle, and undercarriage.

It is often said that Queen Elizabeth's corgis represent a spirit of goodwill and friendliness, and this holds true for the breed as a whole. Corgis are kind and good-hearted and fairly low maintenance. They are lively and athletic and very playful, subject to what are known as "frantic random acts of play," otherwise known as *frapping*. Their coats are short and easy to groom but prone to shedding. Owners have been known to gather enough fur to knit an entire sweater! Corgis are polite to guests but, being wary of strangers, make good watchdogs.

Bear in mind that they are fundamentally

working dogs. If you don't keep them busy and interested, they may wind up finding "jobs" of their own to do, like nippily "herding" cats, birds, and small children, or, perhaps, digging up gardens. But corgis take to obedience training well, and corgis taught to obey will most likely stay out of mischief. Some people say that corgis are noisy little yappers (the queen prefers to call it "canine barking"), but if you love your corgis and make an effort to include them in family activities, they'll find a happy place in your home.

For information about rescuing a corgi, go to these sites:

- pwcca.org/about-pembrokes/pwc-rescue -network
- cardiganrescue.org

Princess Elizabeth in 1944—the year she received Susan as a gift for her eighteenth birthday

Queen Elizabeth with her three children in 1953 (from left to right): Anne, Charles—and Susan!

The queen and her "moving carpet" of corgis in Liverpool Street Station, London, in 1968

Queen Elizabeth visits with an old acquaintance—Watney, a dorgi bred by Her Majesty—in 1998.

Two handsome gents—Peabody (left) and Mr. Neville (right)—patiently await their walk. While perhaps not of royal lineage, there is nothing "common" about any corgi!